W9-BCA-257

To: Sadie
Love
09/21/14

The Mystery of The Magical
Bwa Bwa Fruit
70
By Devon Kondaks

WinzlowNation, LLC
5625 N Post Road, Suite #103, Indianapolis, IN 46216

The Mystery of the Magical Bwa Bwa Fruit

www.winzlownation.com

Second WinzlowNation Hardcover Edition April 2016

Author/Illustrated by Devon Kondaki

Graphic Design by Rick Lostutter

Printed in China

Library of Congress Control Number: 2 0 1 4 9 1 3 8 2 4

Library of Congress Cataloging-in-Publication Data is available.

ISBN: 978-0-9911083-3-6

DEDICATED TO
MY PARENTS,
DARIUS & CARA

WWW.WINZLOW

NATION.com

Diversity

[dih-vur-si-tee, duh-ver-city]

Noun: Diversity; Adjective: Diverse

def. The range of attributes and gifts that make a creature unique and special.

One beautiful afternoon, Winzlow and Grimble Crumble were relaxing in a meadow in WinzlowNation, when all of a sudden, they spotted something in the distance.

As they approached the object, they realized it was a strange, glowing fruit. Before Winzlow had a chance to inspect the unusual fruit, Grimble Crumble swallowed it whole!

Within seconds, Grimble Crumble's skin turned to all the colors of the rainbow and began to glow!

"Oh, no! How am I going to get my skin color to stop glowing?" pleaded Grimble Crumble. "Why don't we go ask my brother, Doug, at the Gnomtonia Library?" suggested Winzlow. "I'm sure he will have an idea to help you."

GNOMTONIA
So Winzlow and Grimble Crumble began their journey to the Gnomtonia Library, hiking over large hills and tall mountains...

...across raging rivers and streams.

They even tiptoed through spooky caves.

Finally, they arrived in Gnomtonia and headed for the library to find Doug.

When Winzlow and Grimble Crumble found Doug in the Gnomtonia Library, they told him what had happened and asked if he could help.

DOUG
“I have the perfect book!” proclaimed Doug. “It features all types of unusual fruits. According to your symptoms, it seems that you ate a magical Bwa Bwa fruit. The only way to get rid of your glow is to eat a variety of other fruits.”

So the three set out to find fruits by exploring WinzlowNation.

They traveled to the
Banana Islands.

They gathered apples at an orchard,

and climbed peaks to reach pear trees.

They squished grapes at
vineyards in Villa De Lily,

and ate oranges in a grove.

They picked blueberries
at the Royal Estates,

and scaled cliffs to reach peach trees.

After collecting fruits representing each new color of his skin, Grimble Crumble ate them all.

Then, just like that, Grimble Crumble's glow disappeared! "Thanks for all the help!" exclaimed Grimble Crumble. "I don't know what I would have done without you."

"We love you no matter what," said Winzlow.
"It's about what's in your heart that
matters most."

The end.